For Vanessa
J. E.

For Joe and Maddy with all my love
P. N.

First published 2020 by Walker Books Ltd
87 Vauxhall Walk, London SE11 5HJ

2 4 6 8 10 9 7 5 3 1

Text © 2020 Jonathan Emmett
Illustrations © 2020 Polly Noakes

The right of Jonathan Emmett and Polly Noakes to be identified as author and illustrator respectively of this work has been asserted by them in accordance with the Copyright, Designs and Patents Act 1988

This book has been typeset in Mrs Ant

Printed in China

British Library Cataloguing in Publication Data:
a catalogue record for this book is available from the British Library

ISBN 978-1-4063-8170-2

www.walker.co.uk

A Present for Rosy

Jonathan Emmett

illustrated by Polly Noakes

Rosy and Rory were the unlikeliest of friends.
They were as different as the sun and the rain.
Rosy was dainty and delicate, while Rory
was big and burly. But they both
loved to explore and discover.

And, because they were different,
they could explore further
and discover more.

Rosy showed Rory
things that only
a bird would
know about ...

like the big white flowers
that blossomed above the trees.

And Rory showed Rosy things that only
a bear would know about ...

like the bright blue beetles that
lived beneath the rocks.

When Rory was bored,
Rosy could always
find something
to interest him.

And when Rosy was sad, Rory could always
find something to cheer her up.

One sunny afternoon Rosy
found Rory dozing in his cave.
"Rory, come quickly," she said.
"What is it?" asked Rory.
"Come and you'll see," said Rosy.

Rosy led Rory to the big rock
that towered above the forest.
"It's too high for me to climb,"
said Rory, shaking his head.
"I can't come with you."
"Yes you can!" said Rosy.
"I'll show you."

And she guided Rory up
and around the rock, until
he reached the very top.

"You're just in time," said Rosy, landing on
Rory's shoulder. "Look!"
Far, far away, in the west, the sun was setting,
filling the sky with extraordinary colours.

It was the most beautiful thing
Rory had ever seen.

Rory wanted to find something
just as wonderful to show to Rosy.
Over the next few days he wandered
all over the forest, searching day ...

and night ...

for just the right thing.

As the days turned into weeks, Rory
kept on searching, but nothing was as
beautiful as the sunset on the big rock.

Rory often climbed to the top of the big rock,
now that Rosy had shown him the way. He was
there early one sunny morning when it began to rain.

He was about to leave when he
saw something extraordinary.
It was not a sunset, but it
was just as wonderful.
This is it, he thought.
This is what I should
show Rosy!

"Rosy, come quickly,"
called Rory, shaking
Rosy's tree gently.
"What is it?"
asked Rosy.

"Come and you'll see," said Rory.
But Rosy did not want to come.
She did not know why Rory had been
away for so long and, while he was
gone, she had grown very sad and lonely.
"It's raining," said Rosy, "and I don't
feel like going out today."
Rory was worried that if Rosy
didn't come soon, it would
be too late.

"Come on, Rosy!" he said.
And he shook the tree so hard
that Rosy fell out of her nest.

Rosy landed with a thump on the forest floor.
She was not hurt, but she was very upset.

Rory was also upset.
"I'm sorry," he said.
He tried to pick up Rosy,
but she flew away
without saying a word.

And so Rosy and Rory
stopped exploring together.

Rosy kept to the treetops and if
she saw Rory in the forest below her,
she turned around and flew another way.

Then one afternoon, Rosy flew to the
big rock and saw Rory sitting there
on his own. And, although she was
still sad, she realised how
much she missed him.

So, instead of turning around, she landed by his side.
"It looks like it will rain," said Rosy quietly.
Rory had been feeling sad too, but his face
lit up when he saw Rosy.

"I know," he said. "You're just in time."
"In time for what?" asked Rosy.
"Stay and you'll see," said Rory.

So Rosy stayed.

And – when it started to rain – she saw!
"This is what I wanted to show you," said Rory.
"It only happens when the sun and the rain
are together," he explained.

Rosy and Rory were the unlikeliest of friends.
They were as different as the sun and the rain.
But sometimes when the sun and
the rain are together ...

they make something

wonderful!

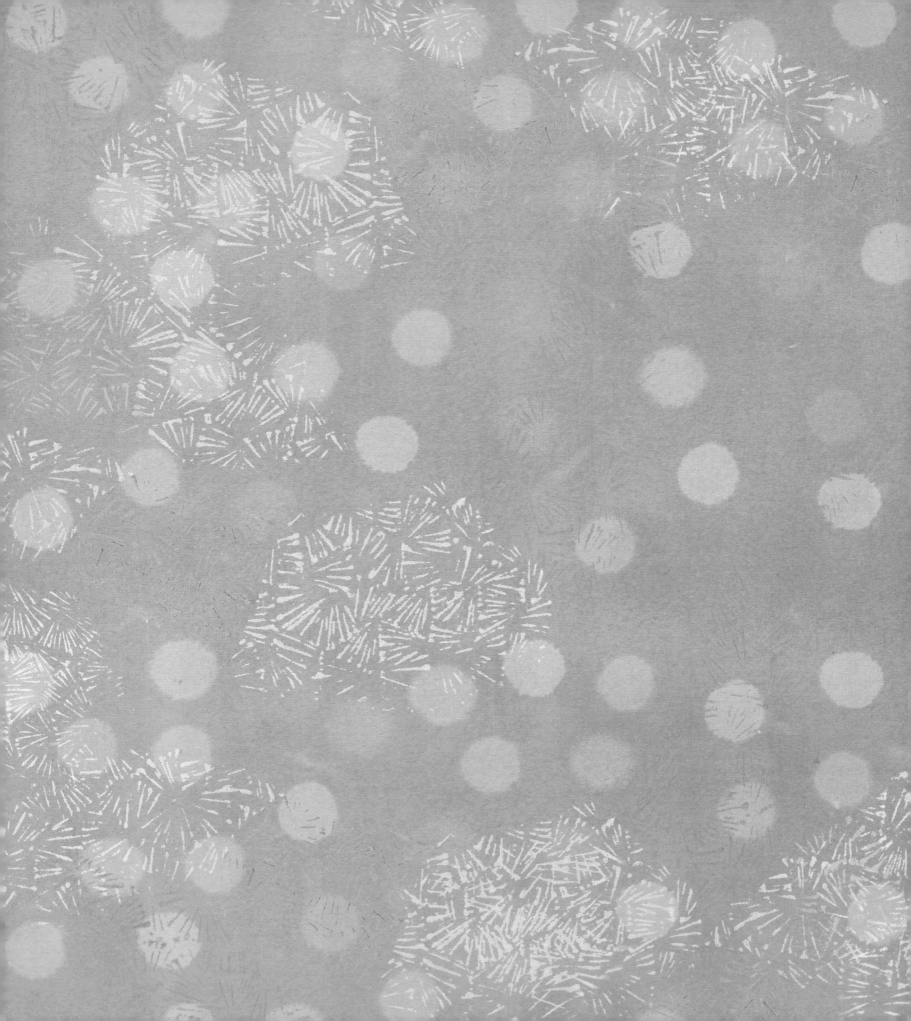